God Painted Me

ISBN 978-1-64299-361-5 (paperback)
ISBN 978-1-64299-362-2 (digital)

Christian Faith Publishing, Inc.
832 Park Avenue
Meadville, PA 16335
www.christianfaithpublishing.com

Printed in the United States of America

God Painted Me

CAROL BAUMAN

Mason always had a hard time falling asleep. His mommy would snuggle and cuddle him until Mason would finally fall asleep.

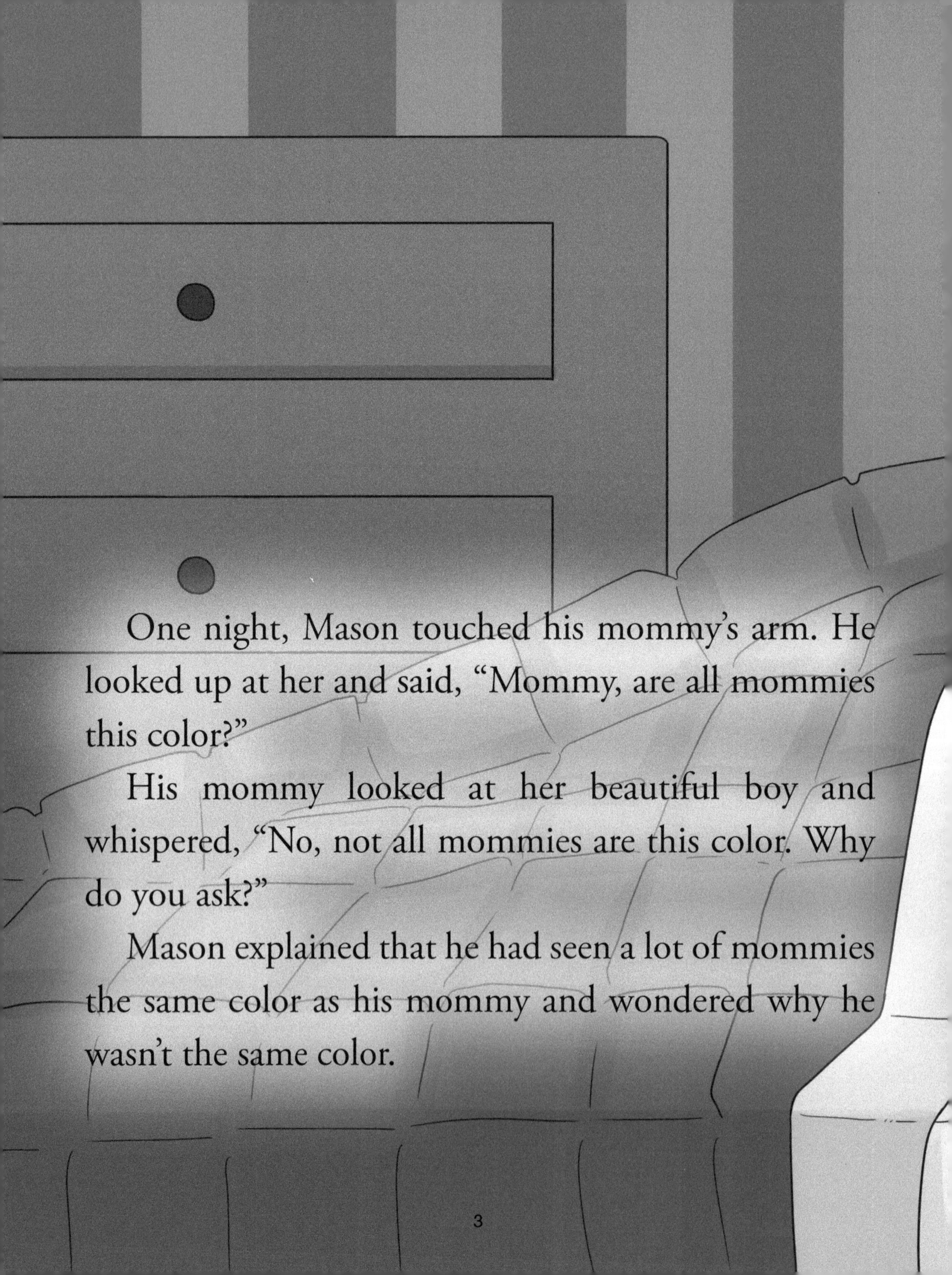

One night, Mason touched his mommy's arm. He looked up at her and said, "Mommy, are all mommies this color?"

His mommy looked at her beautiful boy and whispered, "No, not all mommies are this color. Why do you ask?"

Mason explained that he had seen a lot of mommies the same color as his mommy and wondered why he wasn't the same color.

Before Mason's mommy could answer his curious question, Mason quickly sat up in bed and said, "I know! God painted you that color, and he painted me this color. God paints us all kinds of colors!"

Mason's mommy smiled. She touched his face and said, "Yes, God paints us all kinds of different colors, and that is what makes us each so special and unique."

Mason and his mommy talked about how he was adopted. His mommy told him how God painted him in her heart.

Mason smiled. God painted their family, and that made Mason happy.

“I love you, Mommy,” said Mason. “I’m so glad God painted me to be your little boy.”

“Me too,” said Mason’s mommy.

Mason finally fell asleep. He dreamed of all the different things God painted. His dreams were full of colors, just as God had painted them.

Then God said, “Let us make mankind in our image, in our likeness, so that they may rule over the fish in the sea and the birds in the sky, over the livestock and all the wild animals, and over all the creatures that move along the ground”. Genesis 1:26 NIV

About the Author

Carol Bauman lives on a farm in Oklahoma. She is married and has five children. Carol and her husband adopted three biological siblings from Guatemala before having twins.

Their passion for adoption has allowed them to see the miracles of God, and this was further realized through the eyes of their son, Mason.

Carol enjoys serving as co-creator and coordinator of Farm Girl Fair and various philanthropic work. *God Painted Me* is her first book. Carol is known for her insightful and humorously touching blog, The Unlikely Farm Girl, at www.theunlikelyfarmgirl.com.

CPSIA information can be obtained
at www.ICGtesting.com
Printed in the USA
LVHW070314150319
610729LV00001B/5/P